LEVEL FIVE

Cooking on the Front Burner

Stories with More Vowel Pairs

by Sylvia Davison

Illustrations by
Holly Davison

Go Phonics®

A Foundation for Reading, Writing, and Spelling

Go Phonics®

LEVEL FIVE
Cooking on the Front Burner
Stories with More Vowel Pairs

Published by Foundations for Learning, LLC
Copyright © 2000 by Foundations for Learning, LLC
International Standard Book Number: 0-9726479-0-2
Illustrations © 2000 by Holly Davison
2nd printing (revised)—2003

Go Phonics® is a registered trademark of
Foundations for Learning, LLC
PMB 144 • 246 W. Manson Hwy. • Chelan, WA 98816
www.gophonics.com • 1-800-553-5950

Other Level Five Instructional Materials:

Key Word Chart 2
Workbook—More Vowel Pairs
More Vowel Pairs—Card and Board Games
*Word Lists, Categorized by the Basic Sounds
of the English Language* book (a teaching aid)
Teacher's Guide—More Vowel Pairs

Red Flag Words: Certain words within each story will not be decodable
by the student based on what has been taught to date. These words are
in boxes under each title and must be taught prior to reading the story.

Go Phonics® is a comprehensive, teacher developed program that
provides natural and struggling beginning readers with a K-2 foundation for reading (decoding), handwriting, and spelling (encoding).
It also includes grammar, punctuation, comprehension... It especially
addresses the needs of students with dyslexia and other language-
based learning disabilities. **Go Phonics®** is based on, and is compatible
with *Orton-Gillingham* and *Slingerland* methodology for giving sys-
tematic, simultaneous multi-sensory phonics instruction. It features
step-by-step lesson guides, workbooks, and 48 phonics games that
provide the practice and preparation for reading the decodable,
controlled vocabulary stories.

Table of Contents

Raccoons

Have you ever seen a raccoon?
He is a cute little animal with thick,
grayish-tan fur. A streak of black fur
across the eyes makes him
look like a bandit.
His long, furry tail has
five or more black rings.

A raccoon's front paws have long toes
that are just like fingers. A raccoon can
pick things up and turn them over,
just like people do. He uses his paws
to dunk food in the water before
eating it. There is food for raccoons
in the forest. But when homes take
the place of forests, raccoons may raid

4

garbage cans, or eat corn, melon,
and other things from the garden.

This is a true story:

Mrs. Davison's home was on the edge
of a gully. There was a stream
at the bottom of the gully. Sometimes
a wild animal was seen there.

Dan is Mrs. Davison's son.
When he was 20, he and his friend
Cathy came home to visit. While they
were eating they heard something.
Cathy ran to the glass door.

In the bright moonlight they could see
a huge raccoon. She was looking for food.

Cathy loves animals. She got an egg,
a pan of water, and some crackers.
She set them on the back porch.
The raccoon picked up the egg with
her finger-like toes. She cracked it and
ate it. Then she grabbed the crackers,
swished them in the water,
and ate them.

It was fun to see all of this, but Mrs. Davison couldn't help thinking that this wouldn't be the end of it. Dan and Cathy went back to school, but now Mrs. Davison had a nightly visitor.

The next night, the raccoon was back with a baby raccoon. The big one tapped— YES <u>TAPPED</u>, on the sliding glass door, asking for food.

Mrs. Davison set a pan of water and some crackers on the back porch. She began to worry. Soon she might have many more raccoons at the door. Raccoons can smell bad and can get mean. They should not be kept as pets.

Maybe it was a lucky thing that
she had a trip planned. She left
the next day. She was away six weeks.

When she came home it was late
afternoon. The yard looked fine,
but she saw a lot of paw prints
on the sliding glass door.
The raccoons must
have given up when,
night after night,
no one came
to the door.

Mrs. Davison thought, "There's plenty
of fish in the stream. In the forest,
there's plenty of snails, snakes, snake
eggs, grasses, and more. The raccoons
will be much better off living
on foods they can find in the forest."

But that very night, as she sat
on her back porch, she heard the lady
next door say, "Look dear, there are
the raccoons!"

Cooking on the Front Burner

Many years ago, people did their cooking on a wood stove. The stove had a front burner and a back burner. The wood was placed under the front burner. When the wood was burning, the front burner was very hot. The back burner was just warm.

If you wanted to cook something fast,
you cooked it on the front burner.
People would say, "You're cooking
on the front burner," when you were
getting a job done fast. This all
took place long ago.

Bobby Goodman was a first-grader
at Brookside School. The school was
just one block from Bobby's home,
so Bobby could not ride the bus.
His mother walked to school with him
every day. When school was over,
Mrs. Goodman was always there,
waiting to walk Bobby home.

One day, Bobby's mother wasn't there
to pick him up after school. Bobby waited
a while, but still she did not come.
There was nothing to do but head
for home alone.

It was a windy day. Bobby zipped up
his jacket. He wished he had a hood
to pull over his head. He ran home fast.

When Bobby got home, he rushed in
to look for his mother. He was very
alarmed at what he saw. His mother was
on the floor at the bottom of the stairs.
Her eyes were shut, but she was breathing.
Bobby stood there looking at her
for a moment. Then he shook her arm.

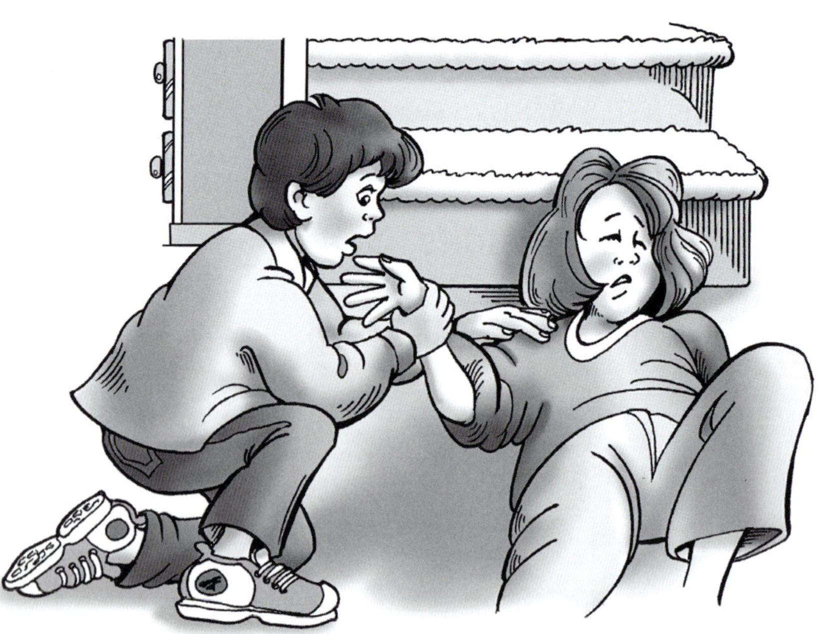

"Mom, Mom, wake up," he cried.
But his mother just lay there. Bobby ran
to the phone and touched 911.
His father's work number was
on a sticker on the phone.
He called that next,
and told his father
what was happening.

In a very short time,
an aid van drove up. Bobby was waiting
at the door. Three men jumped out
of the van and ran inside. They checked
Mrs. Goodman over, and gave her
some smelling salts. She began to
open her eyes. "Where am I?
What's happened?" she cried.

At that moment, Mr. Goodman
came bursting into the room.
"Are you O.K?" he asked.

"She'll be O.K.," said one of the men. "We took care of her."

Mr. Goodman sat beside Mrs. Goodman and gave her a hug.

Mrs. Goodman asked again, "What happened?"

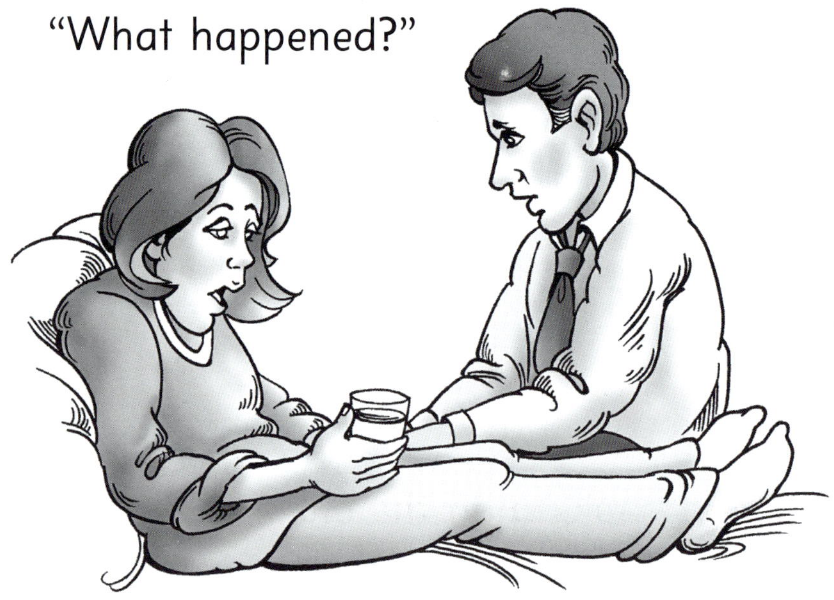

"It looks like you stumbled on the steps and hit your head on the edge of a step. You must have fainted. It's a good thing Bobby called for help right away," said Mr. Goodman.

One of the men was an older man.
He turned to Bobby and said,
"Say, Bobby, you were really cooking
on the front burner."

Bobby had a puzzled look
on his face. The man smiled and said,
"I see you don't understand what
that means." Then he told Bobby
about cooking on the old wood stove,
and about getting jobs done fast.

Ever after this, when Bobby cleaned
his room fast, or Mother fixed a meal
fast, or Father raked leaves fast,
someone would say, "You're cooking
on the front burner."

Snowflakes

It was a cold, wintery morning. The sky was filled with gray clouds. The clouds seemed to be hanging very low. It looked like it might snow.

Ben and Jeff Lowell had been up early. They had had orange juice, a bowl of oatmeal, and some toast. Now they stood with their noses pressed against the window, wishing for snow.

Ben and Jeff loved snow. They loved making a snowman grow big and tall.

They loved throwing snowballs
at each other. They loved
sledding on the hill
near their home.

Becky Lowell loved snow too.
But today, she was very slow
getting up. She had a runny nose
and a slight fever, so she was still
in bed. After a while, she got up
and went to the kitchen. She was
very thirsty. Mom gave her some
orange juice. She was glad to
have that, but she didn't want oatmeal
or toast. Mom looked very worried.

Mom had Becky sit in the armchair. She wrapped her in a blanket, and got a pile of books for Becky to read.

It wasn't long before the snow began to fall. It fell thick and fast. In a short time, there was three inches of snow on everything. Ben and Jeff bundled up in jackets, hats, mittens, and boots, and went out to play in the snow.

Becky could see that Ben
and Jeff were having lots of fun.
"I'm feeling better, Mom," she said,
as she hopped out of the armchair.
"I want to go out in the snow."

Mom felt her head. It was
a bit warm. "No, Becky," she said.
"You still have a fever." Tears began
to flow from Becky's eyes.

Mom was
thinking very hard.
"I have a surprise for you,"
she said. She went over to the desk
and came back with a pile
of thin writing paper and a compass.

A compass is used to make circles.
It has two legs that stretch apart.
One leg has a sharp pin. The other leg
has a pencil on it.

Mom set to work while Becky
watched. She set the sharp pin
in the middle of a sheet of paper.
Then she stretched the compass
so the legs were apart,
and the pencil was near
the edge of the paper.

She tightened the compass.
Then she moved the leg with the pencil
and made a circle.

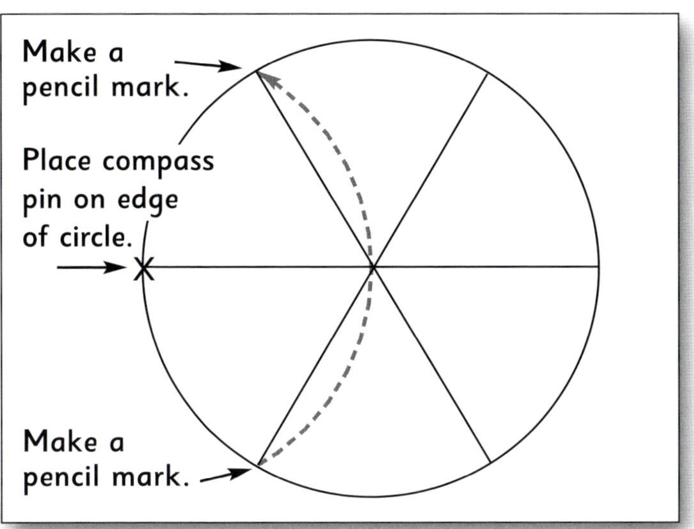

Next, she set the sharp pin on the edge
of the circle. She made a mark on the
circle with the pencil. Then, she put
the sharp pin on that pencil mark,
and made another mark. She did that
until there were six marks on the circle.
With a pencil, she made lines
from each dot to the center, then
to the dot on the other side.

"It looks like a pie
cut into six servings," said Becky.

Mom cut the circle and carefully
folded on the lines. "Now it looks
like one serving of pie,"
said Becky.

Mom folded one more time.
She cut a curvy shape
on the curved edge.
Then she cut into
the folded edges,
going part way across.

Now it was time to show Becky
the surprise. Mom unfolded the paper.
"Oh," said Becky. "It's a snowflake."

Mom explained that all snowflakes
had to be six-sided. Mom and Becky
made lots of snowflakes. There were
no two alike. That's the way it is
with REAL snowflakes, — no two alike.

They put them on the window
with bits of tape. What a pretty sight
that was!

It wasn't long before the days
got warmer and the snow melted.
But indoors, the pretty snowflakes
stayed on the window.

One spring morning, Becky looked
out the window. She could see blossoms
on the apple tree. "Mom," she said,
"I think we should take the snowflakes
off the window. It's spring!"

As they put the snowflakes away,
Becky said, "Making the snowflakes
was as much fun as playing with
real snowflakes."

"And they lasted a lot longer,"
said Mom with a smile.

The Shoemaker

Fred Bower was a shoemaker.

He was a very good shoemaker.

He and his wife, Greta, lived

in a little apartment behind his shop.

The Bowers had lived in the same place

for many years. Fred had made

a good living making shoes

for the people in town.

Now Fred Bower had fallen on hard
times. He had been ill for many weeks.
He had not been able to make shoes.
He had no money. There was leather
for just one pair of shoes, but he was
too sick to make them.

Before long, Fred became so sick
that Greta took him to the hospital.

"How am I going to make shoes?"
moaned Fred. "I MUST make shoes.
We have no more money."

"We'll think about that
when you get well," said Greta.

On the street behind the shoe shop
lived Old Grandpa Dowd.
He had lived there for many years.
He had become a good friend
to the Bowers.

Old Grandpa Dowd had never
told the Bowers this, but once he too
had made shoes. When he heard
of Fred's problem he thought,
"Maybe I can help my friends."

While Fred was in the hospital,
Old Grandpa Dowd went to Fred's
shop. He saw the leather on the shelf,
and set about making a pair of shoes.
They were very nice looking,
and seemed to be very well made.
He set the shoes in the shop window.

After a short stay in the hospital,
Fred and Greta came home.
The doctors had taken care of Fred's
illness. With rest and good food
he would soon feel fine again.

When Fred and Greta got home,
they were surprised to see a pair
of shoes in the shop window.
"What is this?" cried Fred. He put
the shoes on. They looked grand!
But when he tried
to walk in them they
had a BIG *squeak*.

"Who did this?" cried the shoemaker
with a frown. "Someone tried to help
us. But now we have a pair of shoes
we cannot sell." They set the shoes
back in the window. They were very sad.

Fred and Greta were so upset that they didn't hear the crowd coming down the street. The circus had come to town. The clowns were marching down the street to let everyone know. They were inviting people to come to the show.

One of the clowns happened to see the shoe shop. He saw the shoes in the window. The clown stepped out of line and went into the shop. Fred and Greta were so sad they couldn't even greet him.

"Say," said the clown
with the smile that never went away.
"I see you have a pair of shoes
in your window. I need a pair of shoes.
Mine are very old and falling apart.
But there's a problem. Clown shoes
have to squeak. Can you make those
shoes squeak?"

Frowns turned to smiles as Fred said,
"No problem!"

With the money the clown paid
for the shoes, Fred was able to buy
leather for five more pairs of shoes.
It looked like Fred's worries were over.

It was a while before Fred and Greta
learned that Old Grandpa Dowd
had made the squeaky pair of shoes.
They thanked him for his kind help.

When winter came, it was Grandpa
who needed help. He had a bad cold.
Greta knitted him a warm hat, scarf,
and mittens. Fred made him a pair of
warm boots. Then, with hot chowder
and muffins, Fred and Greta called on
Old Grandpa Dowd.

After warm hugs
and a big THANK-YOU,
they all sat down at the table
and had lunch together.

A Mouse
in Our House

Pete, a twelve-year-old, lived
in the town of Mount Vernon with his
mom and dad. Pete was a match box
car collector. Match box cars
are tiny cars about two inches long.

    In the summer, Pete earned money
by mowing grass. He worked
in his yard as well as other yards.
He earned lots of money. He saved part
of it. Part, he spent on match box cars.

    Pete made many trips to the store.
Each time he would come home
with another car for his collection.
Each time he would unwrap the car
and throw the wrappings in his
wastebasket. His wastebasket was
a large woven basket. It sat beside
his desk in front of the heat outlet.

When fall came, the days were
cloudy and cooler. Dad turned
the furnace on so the house would
be warm.

Pete didn't have many mowing jobs
now. Once in a while he got
outdoor jobs raking leaves and
cleaning yards. He did not make
as many trips to the store.
His match box car collection
got bigger, but very slowly.

Pete sat down at his desk to work
on a book report for school. Soon,
he heard a funny sound—the kind
of sound a mouse might make.
He thought it was coming
from the heat outlet. At first
he didn't give it much thought.

One Saturday, after finishing a job
raking leaves, Pete went to the store.
Again he crumpled up the wrapping
paper and tossed it in the basket.
The new match box car was
put on display.

As Pete worked on his report,
he heard the sound two more times.
"Hm," he thought. "I wonder if
a mouse has come in out of the cold.
He may be down there
in the heat outlet."

When he heard the sound
three more times, he called to Mom.
"Mom, I think we have a mouse
in our house."

Mom came rushing in. "Nonsense,"
she said. "We have lived in this house
for ten years. We have NEVER had
a mouse in our house."

"But I keep hearing this sound,"
said Pete. "It's coming from the part
of the room where the heat outlet is.
I think there's a mouse down there."

"I have a plan," said Mom.
"First let's close the door and put
a blanket at the bottom.
Then the mouse can't get away."

"Done!" said Pete.

"Now," said Mom. "We'll sit still
on the floor without making a sound."

Mom was rather stout,
but she got on the floor and
tucked her knees under her chin.

Pete sat beside her. It wasn't easy,
but they sat there without moving
for quite a while.

Then it happened. Just as
the furnace turned on, they heard
a squeaky sound. With eyes and ears
wide open, they sat still a while longer.
No mouse came out.

Mom and Pete got closer
to the heat outlet. It happened again.
The squeaky sound came just as
the furnace turned on. Mom and Pete's
mouths dropped open. The warm air
from the furnace was blowing through
the holes in the wastebasket. The air
made the crumpled paper move.
THAT was the squeaky sound.

Mom and Pete
laughed their heads off.
"THAT'S the mouse in our house,"
giggled Pete, "some crumpled up paper."
"Well," said Mom, still laughing.
"We're a pretty good pair of detectives!"

Everything Old is New

Carl Stewart and Ann Cooper were born and raised in the midwest. They both lived on farms. Their farms were "next door" to each other. That means they were a mile or so apart, with no other farms in between.

Ann's father raised sheep. Her mother spun the wool into yarn, and used the yarn to weave cloth on her loom.

The farms were not modern.

They had to pump water from wells.

They grew their own vegetables.

Both farms had cows and chickens.

Ann and Carl spent many hours

harvesting vegetables, milking cows,

and gathering chicken eggs.

Carl's father grew a lot of wheat and corn. He would grind the grains into flour or cornmeal. When Carl's mother made johnnycake with fresh ground cornmeal, it was a real treat.

Carl's mother was an expert at braiding rugs. Carl helped her by cutting cloth into long strips.

When Carl and Ann completed their schooling, they were married.

Carl's job took him to New York City. He and Ann both missed the farm life, but there was nothing they could do about it.

So Mr. and Mrs. Stewart lived in New York City for many years. They had two children. Now they were grown up and married, and had children of their own. There were seven grandchildren.

Carl and Ann Stewart often talked about their life on the farm as children. They sometimes dreamed that it would be nice to go back to that kind of life. But they knew that might never happen.

It was time for Carl Stewart to retire from his job. They decided to take a trip around the New England states. The fall leaves were a fantastic sight.

As they drove around the state
of Vermont, they happened to see
a house for sale. It was an old
farmhouse with quite a bit of land.
There was a barn and some other
buildings. There were some huge
maple trees. Both their faces lit up
and both spoke at once as they said,
"This would be a great place to retire."

The Stewarts sold their New York
apartment and moved to Vermont.

The farm house was modern,
with running water, a gas furnace,
and electric lights. They decided to make
the other buildings like the ones they
remembered from childhood. Their dream
was coming true, and it grew.

The Stewarts hired a crew to work
on the buildings. It took a few months
to complete the job.

In the largest building, a loft
was built. A ladder went up to the loft.
Cots were set up there, making a place
for people to sleep.
On the main floor,
the Stewarts set up
a **spinning wheel**
and **loom**.

In one of the smaller buildings
they put an **old wood stove**.
A table was put in the middle
of the room. On the table was a mortar
and pestle. These would be used
to **grind corn** into cornmeal.

There was a jar for **churning butter**.
The jar had a lid with a handle on top.
Paddles were attached to the lid
to churn the cream.

The Stewarts had moved here
in the fall. Now it was spring,
and soon school would be out.
They wrote notes to their seven
grandchildren inviting them to visit
their farm for a few weeks. The children
were delighted. They flew to a nearby
airport where their grandparents
met them.

When the children got to their
grandparents' home, they were
very surprised to see that everything
was OLD. But it was all NEW to them.

The children slept on cots in the loft
of the large building. On the main floor
they all braided strips of cloth and
sewed them together to make a rug.

Bayberry bushes grew nearby.
Berries from these bushes were used
to make nice-smelling candles.

In one of the smaller buildings,
the children learned to dip candles.
It took quite a long time. A string
had to be dipped into hot wax,
then lifted out to cool a bit.
Then it was dipped again,
and again, and again,
— at least twenty times.
At last they had candles
that were a good size
for burning.

In the other small building,
the children ground corn into meal
and made johnnycake. Then, they put
cream in the glass jar, put the lid on,
and turned the handle. They could see
the paddle spin. The cream turned
into butter. Everyone said that
the johnnycake with butter was
the best thing they had ever tasted!

After the grandchildren left,
the Stewarts began thinking how nice
it would be to have other children
come and visit the farm. They went
to schools in the nearby towns
and talked about their farm.
It wasn't long before children began
coming for day or weekend visits.

The Stewarts called their place
Early Settlers' Farm. From time
to time they added to their dream.

The people in the nearby towns
would ask, "I wonder what's new
at the old farm?" The Stewarts
spent many years living their dream
and showing children many old ways
of doing things. The children were
never bored, because everything OLD
was NEW to them.

Awful or Awesome?

| half   full   national   answer |
| breakfast   wonder |

The car was loaded, and Shawn and Kristy Brewster were excited. School was out. The next morning they were going on a trip to visit some national parks in the west.

The Brewsters live in Lawton, North Dakota. Mr. and Mrs. Brewster were high school teachers there.

The family wanted an early start, so they were up at dawn. They'd stop for breakfast on the way.

Shawn walked across the lawn to get in the car. He was yawning.

"This is awful.
I don't like getting up so early."
said Shawn.

"Well," said Mom. "Rather than
think about bad things, let's think
about good ones. Getting up at dawn
means we'll see the sunrise. Look,
the sky is full of color. It's awesome!"

That remark started a big discussion. "Mom," said Kristy. "Shawn just said this is awful. Then you said the sunrise was awesome. You both used the word **awe**, but he was thinking bad things, and you were thinking good things. I don't get it."

Since Mom was an English teacher, she began to explain. "Well," she said. "When you add the suffix **ful** to a word, it means *full of*, or *lots of*. *Thankful* means full of thanks. When you add the suffix **some** to a word, it also means *full of*, or *lots of*. *Fearsome* means *full of fear*."

"The way you're explaining it, Mom, *awful* and *awesome* mean the same thing," said Kristy.

"Except for one thing," answered Mom.

"*Awe* is a funny word. It has
two meanings that are almost opposite.
It means *wonder*, and it also means *fear*.
Most of the time, people use the word
awesome for wonderful things, and
the word *awful* for fearful or bad things."

"O.K.," said Shawn. Let's practice
using both words on this trip.
I'll start by saying I feel awful."

"Are you getting sick?" asked Mom.

"No," said Shawn "I'm just hungry."

"So, let's stop for breakfast," said Dad.

They spotted a nice diner
and stopped to eat. Everyone ordered
the same thing—fresh orange juice,
Swedish pancakes with maple syrup,
and bacon.

"That was an awesome meal,"
said Dad. That made everyone smile.

The Brewsters headed west and
made their first stop at Theodore
Roosevelt National Park. The name
"Badlands" is often given to this park.

Shawn and Kristy thought that was
a good name. When they looked out
at the jagged peaks and sandy ridges,
they felt they had landed on the moon.
They both thought it was awful.
The awesome part happened
when they saw an eagle flying overhead.

Even more awesome was the sight
of a herd of pronghorns. Shawn said,
"I bet they could beat us if they ran
alongside our car on the highway."

pronghorn deer

"You're right," said Dad. "Pronghorns are the fastest running animals in North America."

As they left the park, they stopped the car to watch a doe and her fawns cross the road.

"Look at their funny long ears," said Dad. "That must be why they're called mule deer."

Heading for South Dakota, they drove through the Black Hills National Forest. These are foothills with old pine.

Shawn and Kristy didn't think these hills
were exciting, yet they weren't awful.
But, they were about to see
an awesome sight they'd never forget.

They reached Mount Rushmore.
This is a mountain on which are carved
the faces of four presidents. Each face is
about sixty feet high, about three times
as tall as a one-story house.
The faces seemed almost alive.

The next part of their trip was
through Custer State Park. They drove
the Wildlife Loop Road. Mom and Dad
said they would have to stay in the van.
Shawn thought that was awful.
But when he saw the herd of bison
grazing in the grasslands,
he understood. These awesome beasts
are six feet tall, and best watched
from the safety of the car.

They had time for one more stop.
They chose to go to Jewel Cave.
The cave was damp and cold.
That part was awful. The crystals
hanging in the cave, sparkling
like jewels, were awesome.

Coming out of the cave, the Brewsters
were happy to feel the warm sunshine.
They felt it was **awful** that their trip
was ending so soon. But they had seen
many **AWESOME** sights.

The Haunted House

The old two-story house
on Hawthorn Street had been empty
for a long time. The owner,
Laura Benson, had died of old age.
Her daughter lived in Australia.
She was not interested in keeping
the house. Now a FOR SALE sign was
in the middle of the overgrown lawn.

Two blocks from this house was
the Evergreen School. Children who
lived on Hawthorn Street walked past
the old house every day on their way
to school. At first, this didn't seem to
bother anyone. But with the passage
of time, things began to change.
The once lovely yard became unkempt.
Here and there, the paint was peeling,
and there were some cracked windows.
The old house began to look scary.

One day, as Luke and Paul Austin
walked past the old house, they heard
a loud tapping sound. They walked
just a little faster. When they got home,
they hurried into the house. Mrs. Austin
was folding laundry. She could see
that the boys were upset.

"We heard some tapping sounds coming from the old house," said Luke.

"That house is haunted," said Paul.

"No," said their mother. "I'm sure the sound can be explained."

The boys kept hearing the sounds, and other children were hearing them. The fathers of the children walked around the outside of the house, but could find nothing wrong.

One Friday, all the children stayed after school for a basketball game. As they started home, it was beginning to get dark. When they passed the old house, they heard a sound that made their flesh creep. It was a wailing sound, almost like a baby crying. Luke ran lickety-split down the street.

"Stop," yelled Paul. "You're supposed to wait for me."

Luke ran so fast that he tripped and scraped his knee. He began to cry. Paul caught up with him and helped him home.

"What happened?" asked their mother. "Paul, you're supposed to take care of your little brother!"

"It's not my fault," said Paul.
"We heard a wailing sound coming
from the old house. Luke got so scared
that he started to run fast. I couldn't
stop him. That house IS haunted."

Again, the fathers of the children
walked around the house. Again,
they could find nothing that would
cause a wailing or tapping sound.
One father was at the back
of the house. He heard some soft,
strange, music sounds. He didn't find
where they came from.

When the children heard that,
they said, "We're not going near
that old house again." From then on,
they went to school the long way—
by going around the block.

That summer, in August, something
happened that caused a change.
An older couple, Dave and Sally
Faulkner, were driving around town.
They had just retired from their jobs.
They were looking for a house they
could turn into a Bed and Breakfast.
That's like a motel, but homier.

They turned onto Hawthorn Street.
When they saw the old house,
they both shouted, "That's it!"

"This is perfect," said Sally.
"It's near bulb farms, the fair grounds,
a national park, and ski slopes."

"There's something to do or see
every season of the year," said Dave.

The Faulkners called the real estate
agent. He met them at the old house.

"Are you sure you want this place?"
he asked. "It's an eyesore,
and the children say it's haunted."

"We can take care of the eyesore
part," said Dave.

"And we don't think there's
such a thing as a haunted house,"
said Sally. "We would like to have
the house inspected."

In a few days an inspector came out
to the old house. He'd heard about
all the strange sounds, and he was set
on finding the cause.

First he walked around the outside
of the house. He looked up to see
a flicker. <u>THERE</u> WAS THAT
TAPPING SOUND!

A flicker is like a woodpecker.
They like to nest under the eaves
of empty houses,—and this flicker
had done just that. They hammer
on wood with their long, sharp beaks.
THAT was the tapping sound
everyone was hearing.

Inside, the inspector found a sturdy,
well-built house. When he went
up in the attic, he was startled
by a barn owl! It must have gotten in
through the broken window
and made its home
in the attic. An owl's hoot,
THAT was the wailing cry
the children heard!

The inspector began to wonder
about the music sounds that one
of the fathers had heard. Just then,
a gust of wind blew through
the broken window. That's when
HE heard the music sounds.

Well, in the corner near the window
was a small harp. When the wind
blew in, it made the harp strings
vibrate. The inspector just stood
there and laughed. He felt like
a pretty good detective.

The Faulkners bought the house.
With brushes, paint, and polish,
they made it look new. In the yard
they hauled away weeds and branches
and planted lots of flowers.

Faulkners' Bed & Breakfast

became the pride of Hawthorn Street.
The mothers and fathers were happy
to be rid of an eyesore. The children
were happy too. They never again
went around the block to get to school.

Noisy Boys

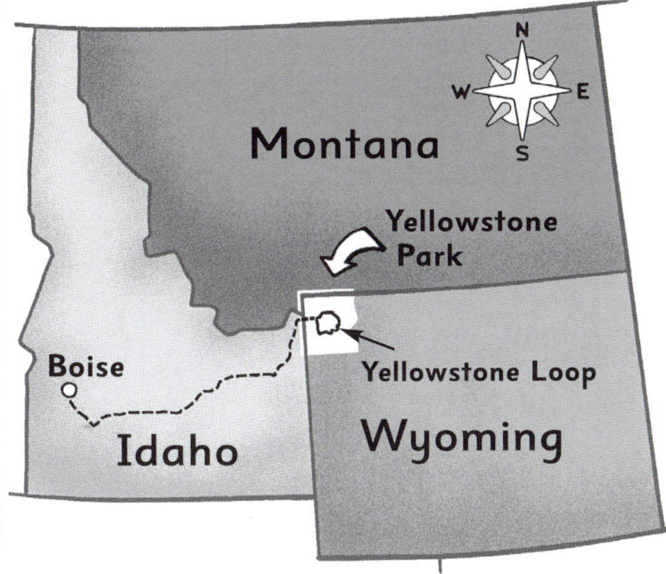

Mr. and Mrs. Joyner and
their three boys were looking forward
to their first camping trip. They lived
in Boise, Idaho, and were planning
to visit **Yellowstone**—the oldest
national park in the United States.
It is in the northwest corner
of Wyoming. A bit of it extends north
into Montana, and west into Idaho.

The Joyner boys were a noisy bunch.
All three were would-be drummers.
At home, Mrs. Joyner sometimes
put on ear plugs. For the camping trip,
the boys were told they would have to
keep the noise down. They didn't want
to disturb other campers. They left
all their noisy toys at home.

The family left Boise and drove east,
then north. They entered **Yellowstone**
at the northwest corner of the park.

Before leaving home, the Joyners had
called the forest service for information.
They were told that it might be cool,
so they would bring warm clothing.
No one could tent-camp in the park
because there was danger of bears.
Since the Joyners had a camper,
that wouldn't be a problem.

They found a good campground.
After driving all day, they were eager
for a good night's rest.

The next morning they started
on "Yellowstone Loop." They planned
to stay at a different campground
each night.

On the first day, they stopped
at **Mammoth Hot Springs**,
with its boiling water.

Next they visited the black-faced **Obsidian Cliff**. This really interested the boys. They learned that long ago, Indians used obsidian for arrowheads.

The next day was the day for geysers. First there was **Norris Geyser**, the hottest spot on the earth. Then there was **Steamboat Geyser** with its plumes of steam rising 380 feet. At the south end of the park was the world-famous **Old Faithful**. This one erupts like clockwork.

As they rounded the south end
of the park and headed north,
the Joyners began to see more birds
and animals. At **Yellowstone Lake**
there were pelicans and honking geese.
Here and there they spotted
moose and elk.

As they went further north,
there were dense forests and waterfalls.

After another day of sight-seeing,
the Joyners parked in their third
campground. For dinner they had
broiled steak with rice and steamed
vegetables. There were pears
for dessert. After dinner, Mr. Joyner
wrapped the garbage in the foil
that had been used for cooking.
He put the garbage in the pail
set out by the forest service.

In the middle of the night,
there was a loud clattering noise.
Mr. Joyner jumped out of bed
and ran to the window. "It's a bear!"
he said, pointing to the window.
In a second, everyone was up.

Camper windows are very small.
Five heads were trying to find
a space to look out. The bear had
knocked off the lid of the garbage
pail. It was tearing apart the foil,
trying to get to the bits of steak.

Five pair of eyes got as big
as saucers as they watched
this huge creature. It was fun
to watch, but then they were afraid
the bear might not go away.

It was then that Mr. Joyner yelled
in a loud voice, "Forget what we said
about not making noise, boys.
Start banging on something,
but be careful not to break anything."

The boys grabbed pots and spoons
and turned them into drums
and drumsticks. Mr. and Mrs. Joyner
joined in. How the boys enjoyed that!

Outside, the bear stood
on his hind legs, took a startled look
all around, and took off.

"Thank goodness for noisy boys,"
said Mrs. Joyner.

The Joyner's last stop was at **Mt. Washburn**. They took a three-mile hike to the summit. Lovely wildflowers grew along the trail, and here and there they were greeted by a bighorn sheep.

At the summit was a fantastic view of the entire park. What a great way to end their trip.

On the way home, the Joyners talked about their trip. Each one told what he or she liked best. Mrs. Joyner liked the wildflowers. Mr. Joyner liked the geysers. The boys? Well, what do you think they liked best? You're right! Seeing that big bear and scaring it off with their noise was the BEST. It was something they would never forget.

Weather Reporter

As a small child, Heather Freeman loved looking at the sky. Each morning she would hop out of bed and run to the window. Then she would look up at the heavens and give her mom and dad a little weather report,— rainy, sunny, or a little of both.

When Heather was old enough
for school, she began to notice that
clouds weren't always the same.
Some were thin and wispy,
like horses' tails. Others were puffy
on top and flat on the bottom —
like huge cauliflowers. These clouds
always had blue sky around them,
and didn't bring rain. The heavy, low,
dark clouds meant rain.

By the time Heather was
in second grade, she began
to see that sun and clouds
were just one small part
of weather. Heat and cold
were also very important.

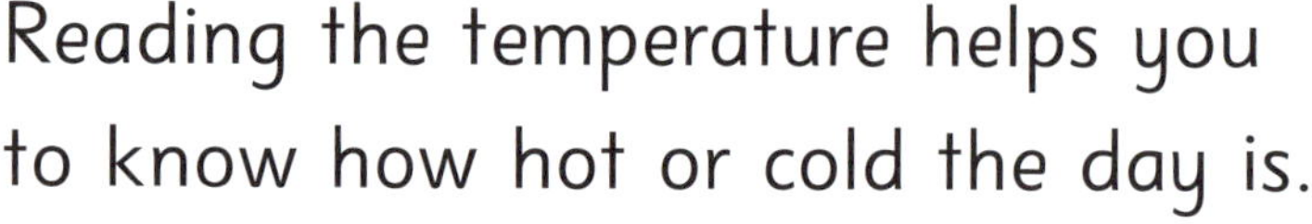

She learned how to
read a thermometer.
It measures temperature.
Reading the temperature helps you
to know how hot or cold the day is.

There are different kinds
of thermometers. In the United States,
we use a Fahrenheit (Fair-en-hite)
thermometer. One day, Heather
learned to write the temperature—**62°F**.
She wrote the number with a little
raised zero after it, followed by
a capital F. The little zero means degrees.

One day, with her mom's help, she used a cooking thermometer to measure three things. First she put it in a glass of ice cubes. It read **32°F**.

Then she let it sit on the kitchen counter for a while. It went to **70°** **F**.

Last, with her mom watching, she put it in a pan of boiling water. It read **212** **°F**. Heather began to understand how temperature affects everything we do.

In second grade, Heather learned
about air. She already knew that air
could be hot or cold. Now she learned
it could be dry or wet. A lot of moisture
in the air meant a humid day.
She learned that air could move
or be still. If it moved a little, it was
a breeze. It could barely move a feather
or some dead leaves. If it moved a lot,
it was a gale.

One day, Heather's dad helped
her make a **wind speed box** to measure
how hard the wind is blowing.
Here is how to make one:

1. Cut off the ends of a shoe box.

2. Cut a slit in the side of the box.

3. Attach a cardboard flap to
   a knitting needle.

4. Push the knitting needle
   through the sides of the box.
   (That end of the box will be pointed
   toward the wind.)

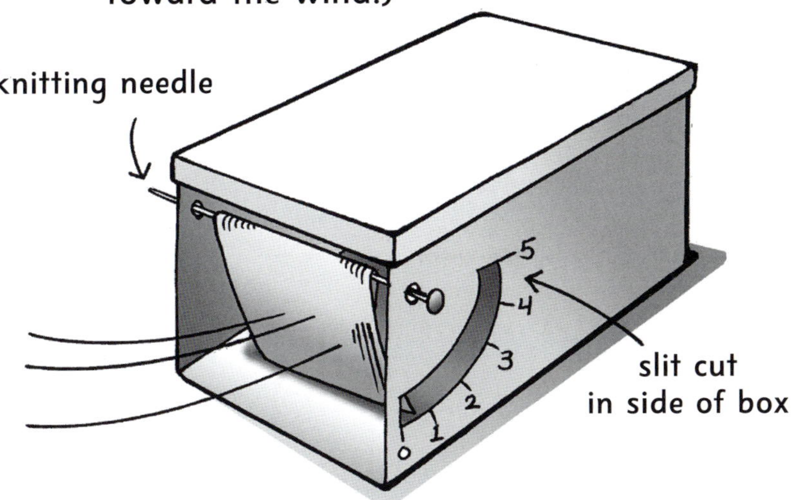

When the wind blows, the flap moves up.

In third grade, Heather learned
about the water cycle. She had seen
puddles dry up after a rain.
She had seen her mom watering
plants in the garden. A few days later,
it had to be done again. Where did the
water go? She wanted to learn more.

One day she put some fresh bread
on the kitchen counter. The next day
it was all dried out (stale).
What happened to the moisture
in the bread?

The next day, Heather and her mom
did a little experiment in the kitchen.
They put water in a pan and put it
on the stove to boil. The water was
disappearing. It was turning into
steam and going into the air.
They held the lid of the pan
upside down and filled it
with ice cubes.
Mom held the lid high
over the rising steam.

When the steam hit the cold lid,
it turned into water drops.
After a short time, the drops got
big and heavy and began to fall.
Heather's eyes got bigger and bigger.
Now she was beginning to understand.
They had just made a little rain shower.

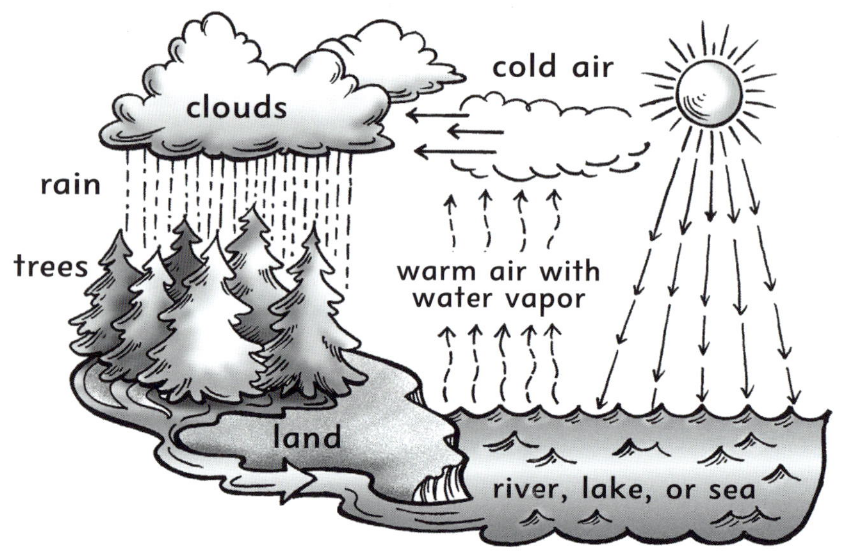

There was so much more to learn
about weather. Heather kept asking
and learning. She visited weather
stations and studied the weather maps
spread on the wall. She listened
to weather forecasts on the news daily.

It was that same year that Heather
started asking about rainbows.
Her grandma gave her a prism.
She explained that sunlight was made
of six colors. Sunlight shining through
the prism was broken up

into six colors. The same thing
happens when sunlight shines
through raindrops. That prism became
one of Heather's dearest treasures.

In school, whenever the teacher
asked a question about weather,
Heather's hand was the first one up.
The children began teasing her.
They called her Heather, the weather
girl. She didn't mind the teasing at all.

Now Heather is twenty-two years old.
She has finished her schooling.
She has a job at the TV station
in her town. What kind of job
do you think she has? You're right!
She's **Heather the Weather Girl**
on the morning news.

Now if you're interested
in the weather, and study as hard
as Heather, perhaps you too can be
a *Heather the Weather Girl.*
And if you're a boy, perhaps you'll be
Dan the Weatherman.

Funny Money

The third-graders in Ms. Bradley's class had just come in from recess. They couldn't help noticing the teacher's desk. It was almost always neat, but now it was cluttered with all kinds of things. There were fishhooks, feathers, stones, seeds, shells, tea, a bag of salt, and a bag of barley.

When all the children were seated, Ms. Bradley said, "Today we're going to talk about trading. But first I have a question for you. What is **money**?"

Chelsey raised her hand. "Money is coins or bills we use to buy things we need or want, or to pay people for things they do for us."

"Exactly," said Ms. Bradley. "We use money to trade for goods and services. We call it **currency**. We haven't always had coins and bills to use in this way."

Ms. Bradley went on to explain. "In early times, people had no currency. They **traded** things they didn't need for things they needed. It's called **bartering**.

"The American Indians and farmers
traded fur for grains. Fishermen traded
fish for wood. As people began
to need and use more things, it was
hard to barter. Suppose a man needed
his chimney cleaned and had a pig
to trade. Even if the chimney sweep
wanted a pig, the job wasn't worth
a whole pig.

"People began to see that they had
to choose one thing for trading.
It was called a **medium of exchange**.
In different parts of the world,
different things were used for trading—
some useful, some not."

Then Ms. Bradley pointed to her desk
and asked, "What do you think this is?"

Stanley raised his hand.
"It looks like a pile of junk to me."
Everyone laughed. No one seemed to
have a better answer than that.

"Well," said Ms. Bradley, "it's money."

"Money?" gasped everyone.

"Yes," she said, pointing to all
the things on the desk as she named
them. "And if I could have gotten

some dogs' teeth, the bristles from
an elephant's tail, some animal fur,
a cow, and a sheep, I could have added
those to my collection. In different parts
of the world, items like this were used
as a medium of exchange.

"For instance, the Mongolians used tea.
The Chinese used salt. People living
near the sea used shells.
What do you think about using
things like this
for money?"

Chelsey raised her hand. "I don't think it was very good. Feathers can blow away, and stones are very heavy."

"Salt may dissolve in the rain, and barley could spoil," said Paula.

Charley asked, "When did they switch to coins?"

Ms. Bradley said, "The earliest coins were made over 2000 years ago in the Kingdom of Lydia, now called Turkey. The coins were a mixture of gold and silver, and ranged in size from 1/4 inch to 1 inch. The bigger the coin, the higher the value."

"That was a good idea," said Cynthia. "When I was little, my uncles were visiting us for Thanksgiving. When we finished dinner, Uncle Jim pulled

two coins out of his pocket—a nickel
and a dime. He asked me to choose one.
I chose the nickel because it was bigger.
Everyone laughed, and I wanted
to run away
and hide."

"Even after money was invented,"
said Ms. Bradley, "lots of people kept
on bartering. People still barter today."

"We do?" everyone asked.

"Don't you trade baseball cards,
marbles, and even toys?" she asked.
Everyone nodded.

"Did everyone use the same money?" asked Charley.

"Every country did its own thing. Today there are about 140 different kinds of currency in use."

"What about paper money?" asked Paula.

"No one knows for sure," said Ms. Bradley. "The Chinese may have been the first to use paper money. It was easy to handle. Today, most money systems include paper money and coins. In our country, in 1790, the United States Congress agreed on the money system we use today. Paper money is printed in Washington D.C..

"The U.S. Mint makes the coins.
The largest mint is in Philadelphia.
I went to school across the street
from that building."

"Did you ever get any free samples?"
asked Stanley. Everyone laughed.

"I have more funny money
to show you," said Ms. Bradley.
She reached into her purse
and pulled out
a checkbook
and a credit card.

"That doesn't look like cash to me,"
said Charley.

"It's cashless money," said Ms. Bradley.
"People put their money in the bank.
They write checks every day to pay
for goods and services. Some people
use credit cards to charge things.
In that way, they can pay later,
and pay for everything at once."

The lesson was over. It was time
to go home. As they lined up,
Stanley was scratching his head.
He had a funny expression
on his face.

"Hm," he said.
"I wonder
what kind of
funny money we'll be using when
we grow up." Everyone laughed.

A Piece of Cake

When someone says the words **a piece of cake**, what do you think of? You may think of a wedge-shaped treat with icing. Maybe there's a scoop of ice cream on the side. But those words are often used in a very different way.

Many years ago, there were dance contests called cakewalks. Couples made up fancy steps. The couple with the best dance won a cake. Later, the term **cakewalk** came to mean something that was fun and easy to do. Later still, the term was changed to **a piece of cake**.

Sayings like this are called clichés (clee-shays). There are thousands of them in the English language.

Just as **a piece of cake** no longer has anything to do with real cake, **brownie points** has nothing to do with chocolate brownies. This expression comes from the Girl Scouts of America. Young girl scouts are called Brownies.

Brownies earn points for projects they complete. Now the term **earning brownie points** is used when someone finishes a job and does it well.

That's the way the cookie crumbles
has nothing to do with cookies.
It means that's how things turned out,
and there's no way they can be changed.

Another cliché that relates to food is
biting off more than you can chew.
It means taking on more jobs than
you can get done.

If you love cherries, your favorite
month of the year must be July.
That's when cherries are in season.
You surely can relate to the cliché—
Life is just a bowl of cherries.
It means everything is just great!
Life really does seem great
when you can eat
all the cherries
you want.

At this point, you may be thinking that all clichés have something to do with food. That isn't so. Many clichés are related to animal traits.

The expression **at a snail's pace** means very slowly. Watching a snail move across the yard will help you understand this saying.

The term **as the crow flies** came into use when someone noticed that crows fly straight to their food. It has come to mean the shortest distance between two points.

A dog with a fierce bark may not intend to hurt you. The saying **His bark is worse than his bite** describes how a person may behave. He or she may scold loudly, but never intend any harm.

Clichés can be based on anything, not just food or animals. The saying **having a field day** was used for army troops going out on special exercises. This same expression is now used when school children are going on a special trip— a trip to a dairy, a pumpkin farm, or maybe the zoo.

You may have enjoyed field trips
more than being in class
doing math or reading. That's how
having a field day has come to mean
taking part in a fun experience.

How about giving someone
a piece of your mind? No, you can't
cut up your brain and give part of it
away. This expression means
speaking up plainly about something
you don't agree with.

There are some silly sounding clichés. One of these is **the whole kit and caboodle**. A *kit* is a collection of things. The word ***caboodle*** comes from the Dutch word ***boedel***. It means household goods. These two words are used together when you want to say you're including everything.

This is just a small sample of the clichés in the English language. Here's hoping that reading them was **a piece of cake** for you. Perhaps, as you read them, you even earned some **brownie points!**

Soup's On!

When it's mealtime, you will often hear the call, "Soup's on!" What do you expect to see on the table? It will most likely be a steaming bowl of cut up vegetables and bits of meat in broth. Maybe there will be some croutons to sprinkle on top of the soup. This is the kind of meal many people enjoy on a wintery day.

In the old days, it was great
to have soup after a sleigh ride.
These days, you might enjoy it
after an afternoon of ice skating
or snowboarding.

But soup is much more than that.
It can have almost any kind of food
in it,—vegetables, meat, fish, grains,
herbs, milk, cream, eggs, and even
fruits. It can be served to begin
a meal, as the main dish, or as
a dessert. It can be served hot or cold.
It can be thick or thin. It can be rich
and high in calories, or it can be
low calorie.

Why do people like soup so much?
Well, for one thing, it can be
cheap to fix.

A good soup stock can be made
with beef or chicken bones that might
otherwise be thrown away. Leftovers
or wilted vegetables in the refrigerator
can be added to the stock. Although
it may have to cook for some time,
it takes only minutes to prepare.
Hot soup can warm you in winter.
Chilled soup can refresh you in summer.

Because soup has been a favorite
meal of people all over the world,
there have been stories written about it.
Soup for the King is one of these tales.

This is a story about a king who
liked soup so much that he wanted
to have it EVERY DAY. The Royal Cook
was not good at fixing soup.
The king HAD to have a cook
who could fix good soup.

The king decided to have
a soup contest. He sent word out
to all the people in the kingdom
over which he reigned.

On the eighth day of the month,
anyone who wished could bring
a tureen of soup to the castle.
The king would sample the soups
and choose a Royal Soup Cook.

When the eighth day of the month
came, a group of cooks gathered
outside the castle gates. Each cook had
a tureen of soup. There were all kinds
of soup, some of them pretty fancy.
At least, their names were fancy.
One cook had **borsch** (borsh)—a soup
made mostly of beets. Another cook
had made **bouillabaisse**
(boul-yob-base)—
a fish soup.

There was one cook with **gazpacho**
(goz-potch-o)—a tomato soup that
is served cold. There were some soups
with funny-sounding names. One cook
brought **boula-boula**. It's green turtle
soup with peas, butter, and cream.

Did you ever hear of **cock-a-leekie**
soup? One cook brought that.
It's made by simmering leeks
with chicken or any kind of fowl.
Sometimes prunes are added.

The cooks were asked to form a line.
The king would see them one at a time.

In a small neighboring village,
just outside the kingdom, lived a poor
widow and her young son. The widow
worked very hard, but she had
very little money. She and her son
had a small garden. The food from
their garden kept them
from starving.

This year, the garden crops had been
fantastic. The crop of potatoes and
leeks was so big, the widow didn't
know how she could use them all.
Then, she had a great idea. She made
a huge pot of potato leek soup.

The pot weighed a lot, so she put it
in a cart and told her son to take it
to the market in the city. The boy was
to sell the soup and use the money
to buy some flour and rice.

On the way to the city, the boy
passed by the castle. He saw the group
of people lining up outside the gates.
He wanted to see what was happening,
so he walked toward the castle.
As soon as he approached the gates,
a guard came over
and told him
to stand at the
end of the line.

"But, but, but," cried the boy, intending to explain where he was going.

"No talking, boy," yelled the guard. "Do as I say." He was so angry that the veins in his neck stuck out. "Just get in line," he ordered.

The frightened boy got in line, not having the least notion of what was happening.

It wasn't long before the boy was ushered into the king's dining room. Someone took the lid off his pot of soup and filled a royal bowl with potato leek soup. The bowl was set before the king. When the king tasted the soup, his face lit up with pleasure.

"You are just a youth," he said to the boy. "Did you make this soup?"

"Nnnno-no Sssss-sir. Mmmm-my mm-mother made it," answered the boy in a trembling voice.

"Well go home and fetch her," ordered the king. "This is the best soup I have ever tasted. I want you and your mother to come and live in the castle. From this day on, she will be the Royal Soup Cook."

What a turn of events that was!
Can you imagine how the poor widow
felt when her son told her the news?

When the widow and her son
returned to the castle, they were given
a royal tour. They were then led
to a lovely apartment near the royal
kitchen. They lived there happily
for many years—cooking soup
for the king.

By the way, the simple potato leek
soup earned a fancy name of its own.
It's called **vichyssoise** (vee-she-swoz).

Now that you have learned

the 42 sounds in

the English Language

and can read MANY words,

you're REALLY cooking

on the front burner!